# Gift & Box

For my grandchildren,
with love from Mimi —E.M.

For Avó Maria —B.M.

THIS IS A BORZOI BOOK PUBLISHED BY ALFRED A. KNOPF

Text copyright © 2023 by Ellen Mayer
Cover art and interior illustrations copyright © 2023 by Brizida Magro

All rights reserved. Published in the United States by Alfred A. Knopf, an imprint of Random House Children's Books,
a division of Penguin Random House LLC, New York.

Knopf, Borzoi Books, and the colophon are registered trademarks of Penguin Random House LLC.

Visit us on the Web! rhcbooks.com

Educators and librarians, for a variety of teaching tools, visit us at RHTeachersLibrarians.com

*Library of Congress Cataloging-in-Publication Data.* Names: Mayer, Ellen, author. | Magro, Brizida, illustrator. Title: Gift & Box / Ellen Mayer ;
[illustrations by] Brizida Magro. Description: First edition. | New York : Alfred A. Knopf, [2023] | Audience: Ages 3–7. | Summary: Gift and Box make way
from Grandma's house, on cars and trucks and ships, to their exciting destination. Identifiers: LCCN 2022047303 (print) | LCCN 2022047304 (ebook) |
ISBN 978-0-593-37761-1 (hardcover) | ISBN 978-0-593-37762-8 (library binding) | ISBN 978-0-593-37763-5 (ebook) |
Subjects: CYAC: Gifts—Fiction. | Boxes—Fiction. | Voyages and travels—Fiction. | LCGFT: Picture books. Classification: LCC PZ7.1.M385 Gi 2023 (print) |
LCC PZ7.1.M385 (ebook) | DDC [E]—dc23

ISBN 978-0-593-81247-1 (proprietary)

The text of this book is set in 16-point Queulat Condensed.
The illustrations were created using rolled printmaking inks, crayons,
handmade stamps, and paper collage, then assembled digitally.
Book design by Nicole Gastonguay

MANUFACTURED IN CHINA
10 9 8 7 6 5 4 3 2 1

Random House Children's Books supports the First Amendment
and celebrates the right to read.

This Imagination Library edition is published by Random House Children's Books, a division of Penguin Random House LLC, exclusively for
Dolly Parton's Imagination Library, a not-for-profit program dedicated to inspire a love of reading and learning, sponsored in part by
The Dollywood Foundation. Penguin Random House's trade editions of this work are available where all books are sold.

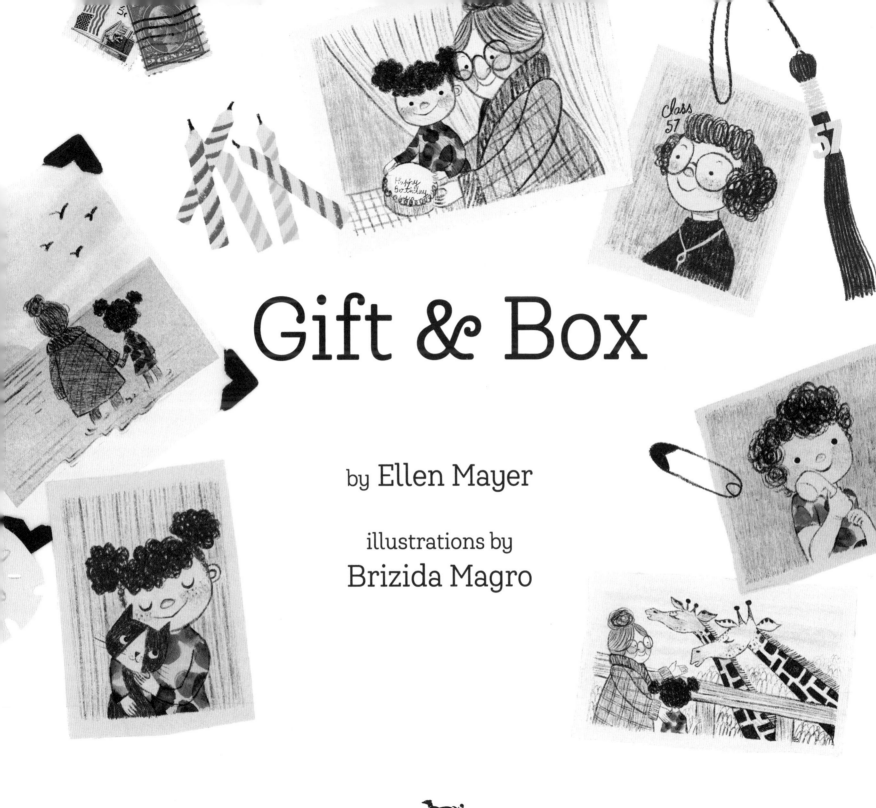

# Gift & Box

by Ellen Mayer

illustrations by
Brizida Magro

ALFRED A. KNOPF
New York

**G**ift was a gift.

Box was a box.

Together they were … a package.

Gift's purpose was to delight.
Box's purpose was to protect.

They were on their way.

The journey ahead was long.
They were not Priority Mail.

Being a package was not always easy.
Sometimes the journey was boring.
"When will we be there?" asked Gift.
"Sit tight," replied Box. "We're still
waiting at the post office."

Sometimes it was bumpy.
"I'm upside down," whined Gift.
"Why don't you practice your
headstands?" suggested Box.

Sometimes it was very scary.
"Where are we now?" asked Gift.
"We're lifting off!" gasped Box.
"HOLD ON!"

Sea spray blew across choppy waves
for days and days.
"I don't feel good," moaned Gift.
"And neither do I," groaned Box.

Truck exhaust spewed out into the city street.

"IT SMELLS BAD IN HERE!" sputtered Gift.
Box sighed.

Gift was not always delightful.
Protecting Gift was often challenging.

Occasionally, being a package was fun.

But the fun could turn frightening.

WHIZZZZZZZ!

FRAGILE

BY AIR MAIL
PAR AVION

THUNK!

THUNK!

THUNK!

"HELP!" shrieked Gift.
"Don't worry!" shouted Box.
"I've got you!"

"I'm not a surprise anymore,"
whimpered Gift.
"That's okay," said Box. "I am sure you
will still delight."
"You think so?" sniffled Gift.
"I know so," said Box. "You will *dazzle*."

"We're almost there!" announced Box.
"I'm going to miss you," whispered Gift.
"I'm going to miss you, too," whispered Box.

THUNK!

"What IS it?" said Sofia.

Gift had finally arrived!

Gift and Box were no longer a package.

RIPPPPPPPP!

Gift had brought delight.
Box had protected Gift.
Their journey had ended.
Their time together was over.

"I'll flatten the box and recycle it," said Mama.
"NO!" said Sofia. "I WANT THE BOX, TOO!"

Gift was no longer a gift.
Box was no longer a box.

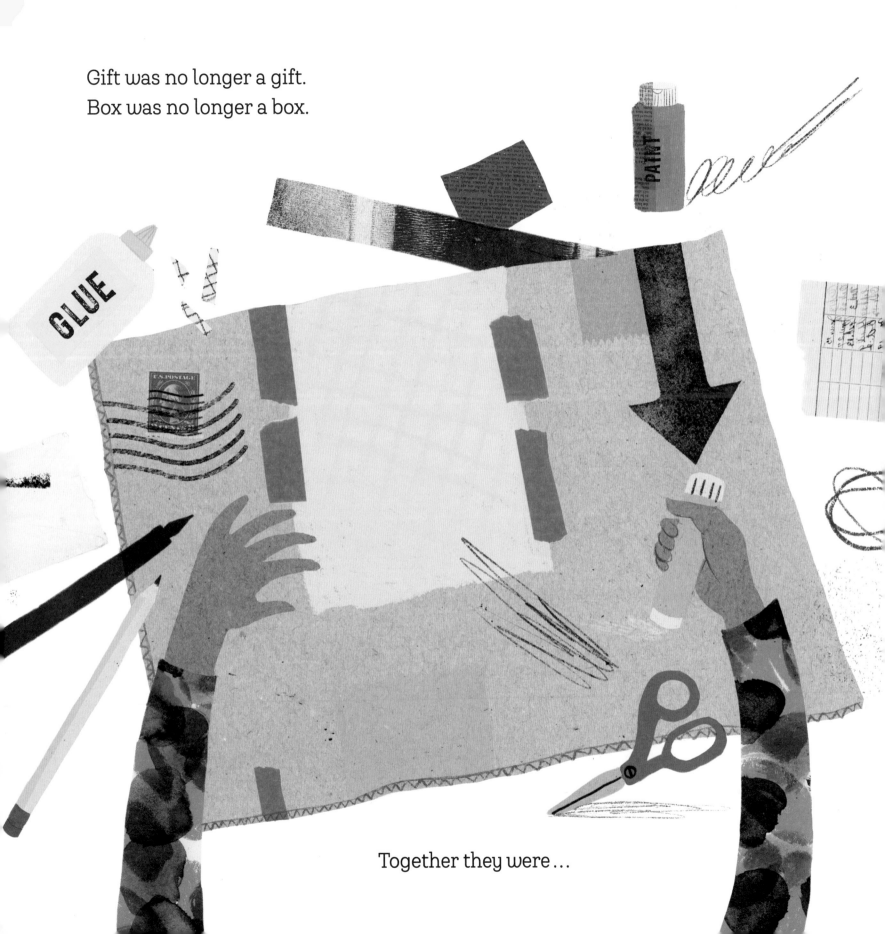

Together they were...

GRANDMA-BOUND

...much more than a package.